Canterbury Tales

Chaucer made modern by Phil Woods
with Michael Bogdanov

D1386671

IRON Press, 5 Marden Terrace, Cullercoats, North Shields,
Northumberland NE30 4PD, UK.
Tel/Fax: 0191 253 1901
email: ironpress@blueyonder.co.uk
www.ironpress.co.uk

First edition 1980: reprinted: 1981, 1983, 1985, 1987, 1990.
This edition first published 1992: reprinted 1996, 2000, 2004 and 2009.

Typeset in Palatino 9pt.

Typeset from disc by Roger Booth Associates.

Printed by Athenaeum Press Ltd, Dukesway, Team Valley, Gateshead.

Amateur: Samuel French Limited, 52 Fitzroy Street, London W1T 5JR
             Tel: 020 7387 9373.
             email: theatre@samuelfrench-london.co.uk

Professional: Elaine Steel, 110 Gloucester Avenue, London NW1 8HX
             Tel: 020 7483 2681
             email: ecmsteel@aol.com

Copies of the music for *Canterbury Tales* obtainable from the above.

IRON Press books are distributed by Central Books
and represented by Inpress Limited, Collingwood Buildings,
38 Collingwood Street, Newcastle upon Tyne, NE1 1JF
Telephone: +44 (0)191 229 9555
www.inpressbooks.co.uk

This version of *Canterbury Tales* by Phil Woods was first presented at the Phoenix Theatre, Leicester on December 19, 1974 with the following cast:

M.C. ....Chris Barnes
Mick Miller ....Micky O Donoughue
Andrew Knight ....Andrew Branch
Nick Franklyn ....Nick Jensen
Heather Bath ....Heather Baskerville
Jenny Cook ....Jenny Whitby
Bev Reeve ....Bev Willis

Music by Chris Barnes and Andrew Branch. Stage Manager Liz Westbrook.
Additional material by Michael Bogdanov and the company.
Directed by Michael Bogdanov.

PHIL WOODS started writing for the theatre in 1970. Since then he has been commissioned to write more than fifty plays. Amongst them, *Show Me the Way to Go Home* (Royal Court Theatre Upstairs), *The Dock* (Hull Truck), *Journeyman Jack* (Liverpool Playhouse), *Arthur Horner* (Foco Novo). Whilst working as Resident Writer with Michael Bogdanov at the Phoenix Theatre, Leicester, he adapted *Canterbury Tales* and *Dracula*. For the New Vic Touring Theatre he also adapted *The Three Musketeers, Sons of the Musketeers, The Last of the Mohicans* and *Frankenstein*. The New Vic produced *Buddy Holly at the Regal* at the Greenwich Theatre and subsequently on a national tour. He lives in County Durham and has written many plays for local companies. *Kiddar s Luck Spain, Northern Glory, Pitmatic Times, Angelo,* and has been associated with Live Theatre, Durham Theatre Company and Newcastle Playhouse. Television work includes *The Forsyte Saga* and 130 episodes for *Coronation Street*.

In performing this version of the Canterbury Tales it should be stressed that we do not for one moment pretend that we are in medieval England. The time is the present and the tales are told in the form of an annual "Geoffrey Chaucer Canterbury Tale-telling Competition." Each of the participants takes charge of his/her own tale. They have adapted and directed it after their own fashion. Thus the Knight's tale might be more elegantly costumed than, say, the Miller's. The music of the Cook's tale might be more harmonic than that in the Reeve's tale, and so on. Between some tales the audience are invited by the M.C. onto the stage to buy refreshments – beer, mulled wine, coffee, mince pies, sandwiches etc.; and members of the company should do their utmost to make everyone feel at home. The requirements of the set are merely those dictated by the location that the director may choose for the production. For instance, it could be a village hall, a marquee, a village green, the backroom of a pub, a theatre, or whatever. There is no reason why costume changes cannot be made on stage, or why the stage-management team should be hidden from the view of the audience. The Miller will tell his own jokes, which must be in keeping with the spirit of the evening, and appropriate to the sensibilities of the audience. It will probably be impracticable to perform all the tales in one evening. Therefore a selection should be made. Ideally, however, the Knight's should open and the Miller's close the show. The running order, whatever the audience may think, is not left to chance. Identical pieces of paper are switched before each draw!

P.W.

Index

M.C: Good evening, ladies and gentlemen. It gives me great pleasure to welcome you to the grand finals of this year's annual Geoffrey Chaucer Canterbury Tale-telling competition. Without further ado, let me introduce you to our finalists. *(Introduces Company, using their real Christian names, e.g. Jeannie Bath, Barry Reeve, Robin Franklyn, Angela Cook etc. One member of the Company, the MILLER (Micky) is sitting in the audience wearing medieval costume, making derogatory remarks about them in turn. (E.g. 'Watch her, she's sex mad' – 'So is he' etc.))*

MILLER: What about me? I'm a finalist.

REEVE: You've been disqualified.

M.C: Ladies and gentlemen. There was to be another tale in the finals, but there were objections from certain quarters *(e.g. some local personage, or Council Committee)* and they threatened to close down the … *(appropriate hall or theatre where the show is being performed)* on account of the Miller's Tale being lacking in common decency and taste. Therefore, I'm afraid, it's been banned.

MILLER: Shame. Good clean muck, my tale.

M.C: This evening's entertainment will take the form of a competition. Each will tell a tale, and at the end I will ask you, the audience, to show your appreciation, while I act as clapometer and will award this cup to the contestant whose tale you most appreciated. Between each tale, you are invited to come onto the stage, where you can purchase mulled wine, beer, sandwiches, mince pies, coffee etc. *(Introduces barman, barmaid etc. MILLER makes more rude remarks)* Please, Micky, could you restrain yourself, while I explain the rules. The names of each contestant have been placed in a hat and Jeannie will ask one of you to select the order in which we perform the tales. We'll do that now, so that we have time to get changed. Judy *(stage manager, introduces her to audience)* could you let Jeannie have the hat. *(JEANNIE asks member of audience to pick a piece of paper. They read out 'The Knight's Tale')* Now, we shall all perform in each other's tale – and anyone misbehaving will be disqualified.

MILLER: What about my tale?

FRANKLIN:	You've already been disqualified.
MILLER:	Well, it doesn't matter if I muck up your tales then, does it? You'll regret disqualifying me.
M.C:	Micky, please, it's very important you take this competition seriously. There's a lot of respectable people in the audience. Well, one or two anyway.
MILLER:	No.
M.C:	What do you mean 'no'?
MILLER:	I've changed my mind. I don't want to be in your boring tales.
M.C. AND OTHERS:	But you must. You can't drop out now. We can't do them without you. *(etc.)*
MILLER:	You should have thought of that before banning my Tale.
REEVE:	Please, Micky. We need you.
MILLER:	*(Eventually)* Alright. On one condition.
M.C:	What's that?
MILLER:	I'll be in your tales, if you let me tell my Top Ten.
M.C:	Top Ten what?
MILLER:	Top Ten medieval mucky stories.
M.C:	Well, I'm not sure about that.
OTHERS:	We'll have to.
MILLER:	*(Producing scroll)* You'll regret this, as well.
M.C:	Careful, Micky. Don't go too far.
MILLER:	Of course not. *(Laughs)* Filthy, all of them.
M.C:	Before we start the Knight's Tale, if anyone would like to get themselves some liquid refreshment would they please

do so now. Quickly.

MILLER: And I'll tell a mucky story. *(Company get ready for Knight's Tale, set props, costumes etc. and help serve drinks, if necessary, or chat to audience. MILLER tells a couple of jokes. M.C. calls for order and asks audience to take their seats.)*

M.C: I will now read what Geoffrey Chaucer said about the Knight. *(Reading from ancient leather-bound tome)*

The Knight's Tale

M.C.:   "A Knight there was, he was a worthy man,
That from the time he first began
To ride a horse, loved chivalry,
Truth and honour, freedom and courtesy.
Gallantly had he fought in many a war
Having travelled the world, no man more.
His worth was valued above all price;
Yet in spite of this he was very wise.
His manner was as gentle as a maid.
Rude words or oaths he never said,
All his life he was most polite,
He was a very perfect gentle-knight."

KNIGHT: Long ago in Ancient Greece, there was a noble Duke named Theseus, his Queen Hyppolita and her beautiful young sister Emily. During a particularly bloody campaign, Theseus found the wounded bodies of two young Theban princes and took them back to Athens, where he imprisoned them in a lofty tower. There was to be no ransom paid for them under any circumstance. From the barred window of their cell all they could see was sky, and part of the royal garden. Thus passed year by year and day by day. Till it happened, one morning in May, young Emily in the garden at the sun's first light went gathering flowers, red and white.
(ARCITE and PALAMON, manacled, are seen in their cell. ARCITE is sitting on the floor. PALAMON walks round and round in a circle)

PALAMON: Arcite?

ARCITE: Yes, Palamon.

PALAMON: I have been pondering the while, the means by which our escape may be realised.

ARCITE: Tell me, cousin, what is the result of your ruminations?

PALAMON: Despair, dear cousin. I fear that never more will we know that blessed state called freedom.

ARCITE: Then keep such thoughts locked carefully in your mind.

Their repetition serves only to increase our sorrow. *(SONG: "COME LOVE WITH ME". EMILY and KNIGHT and M.C. (as Courtiers). EMILY gathers flowers and throws them to Courtiers. PALAMON sees her.)*

PALAMON: Oh!

ARCITE: What ails you, cousin? Your visage has a deathly hue. Your face is white. *(PALAMON sinks to his knees and mumbles).*

PALAMON: Venus, O, Venus. O Fair Goddess. If it be you transfigured in the garden please help us to escape. O, Venus, it must be you, for surely I have beheld the fairest and most beautiful manifestation of woman.

ARCITE: Palamon? Cousin? What is wrong?

CHORUS: "Come love with me and share my happiest hours..." etc.

ARCITE: *(Looks out of window, sees EMILY)* Oh! My heart has been struck as with an arrow. I must see her again. O Palamon, I am in love.

PALAMON: What's that cousin? I'll have none of that. 'Twas I loved her first.

ARCITE: I disagree. You thought she was a goddess. I loved her first as a woman.

PALAMON: Forego such talk, the lady is mine.

ARCITE: To tell the truth, O, Cousin, she is neither thine nor mine and never shall be. We are prisoners here until death we meet, so let's accept our fate and love her each in our own fashion.

PALAMON: Then let it be agreed. We must take turns at the window and maintain our amorous vigil through the day. *(Enter THESEUS)*

THESEUS: Ho, there, young princes. I have this day received a visit of a noble friend of mine. He has pleaded with me to release one of you, that is his kinsman. I have at last succumbed to his desires.

11

PALAMON: Which one, O Duke? Shorten our suspense.

ARCITE: Tell us, please, for good or ill.

THESEUS: The one who has been favoured goes by the name of Arcite. Is that you?

ARCITE: Yes, I am Arcite. My cousin and companion here is Palamon.

THESEUS: He has a sickly hue, yon Palamon. I'll tell you this, young Arcite. Free you may be, but not to walk in any part of my domain. Return immediately to Thebes, never to return here on pain of death. I trust my edict has made itself plain. Come, before I change my mind. *(PALAMON and ARCITE embrace. ARCITE exits with THESEUS)*

KNIGHT: Summer passes, and nights, cold and long,
Doubly increase the anguish strong,
Both of the prisoner and of the lover.
Who's the unhappiest I can't discover.

PALAMON: Oh, woe is me! My pain is double hard to bear. Arcite will surely raise an army and return hither. In my mind's eye I see the object of my love encircled by his arms. While I, a prisoner here remain, devoured by jealousy and rage. Oh, curse the womb that gave me birth. *(ARCITE appears – he has returned to Thebes)*

ARCITE: O, damn the day that ever I was freed. For now I am imprisoned by my love, whom I shall no more see. Would it were Palamon, not I, who was exiled to Thebes. At this moment he is looking at my love, while I am withering away, distracted and deranged. I care no longer if I live or die.
(ARCITE and PALAMON freeze in attitudes of anguish)

KNIGHT: To lovers all, I ask this question;
Who's worse off, Arcite or Palamon?
One sees his lady day by day,
But in a prison must he dwell alway.
For the other the world's an open door
But he shall never see his lady more.

Anguished and alone, Arcite to Thebes returned,

Where pain and awful longing seared and burned
So fierce and strong in him that two years space
Had caused a change complete in voice and face.
The haggard looks that fate-torn love had brought
Arcite saw, and slowly grew the thought...

ARCITE: I've changed completely, even my friends walk by on the other side of the street and don't recognise me. If my friends here don't know me, in Athens I could go completely unmarked. I might even gain the chance of seeing Emily again. I will go to Athens.

KNIGHT: The new Arcite went to Athens straight
And gave it out his name was Philostrate.
He bore himself so well in peace and war
That there was no one Theseus valued more.
Unmarked by Emily Arcite was, it's true.
But for his love there was no cure he knew.
In the dank, dark, impregnable prison
These seven years have tormented Palamon.
Moreover he knows he'll never leave
For to his sentence there's no reprieve.
Who could rhyme in English or scan
His martyrdom? There is no man.
Therefore I'll pass as lightly as I may;
It happened in the seventh year, in May,
That soon after midnight, Palamon,
Helped by a friend, broke from prison
and fled the city with hasty motion.
He'd given his jailer a subtle potion;
A special claret in a porcelain mug
(Miller/Jailer drinks. Smiles)
Mixed with opium and many a Theban drug.

JAILER: Bugger. *(Collapses)*

KNIGHT: That all night long, had he been shaken,
The jailer slept and wouldn't waken;
And thus he fled as best he may.
The night was short and it was nearly day,
And he knew that he must quickly hide
In a grove quite near beside,
(KNIGHT hands PALAMON a potted shrub to hide behind)
Where he could secrete himself all day.
But as chance would have it Arcite passed that way.

13

ARCITE: *(Sings)* "Come love with me and share my happiest hours." O woe! Oh that I have come to this, serving my mortal enemy like an obedient lap-dog. Such is the power of love. Yet I have not received so much as one slight nod from Emily who is the cause of all my woe. Oh, Palamon, my cousin, better had it been we were slain in battle. *(PALAMON jumps out from behind bush)*

PALAMON: And so you shall be, traitor! For seven years I have suffered in my cell whilst you have lived in the company of our Emily. A traitor to your country and our bond, your deception is complete. You counterfeit!

ARCITE: By God in heaven, I'm moved to let your blood. You would prevent me from the dictates of my heart? Why, love is free. There was no bond. So be it, we are honourable both. This disharmony must be settled by recourse to arms. Tomorrow will I come with weaponry – then let us fight to the death. He that wins can seek fair Emily's heart.

PALAMON: Then it is agreed. Give me your hand.

KNIGHT: O, Cupid! Without charitable accord
Your kingdom allows no fellow lord.
It is well said that neither love nor lordship
Will tolerate a moment's friendship.
And so, next morning, before day broke,
He prepared some armour, while no one woke.
And in the grove, the time and place as set,
Arcite and Palamon are now met.
Then a change affects the colour of each face,
As when the hunters in the Kingdom of Thrace,
That standing in a clearing with a spear
While hunting the lion or wild bear,
And hear him charge, rushing through the leaves
Smashing branches; then it is the hunter believes,
Here comes my mortal enemy,
It's death to him or death to me;
For either I must slay him in this clear gap
Else he'll slay me, should I meet mishap.
Similarly the two knights changed colour now
(ARCITE and PALAMON prepare to fight)
Knowing there was no word of greeting, no 'Good Day'
But without rehearsal or any word, straight away
Each gave his help to arm the other,

As friendly as if they were each other's brother.
And after that, with sharp strong spears
They fought, how long? It seemed like years.
(*ARCITE and PALAMON fight*)
You might have thought, to see brave Palamon,
That he was no Knight but an enraged lion.
While Arcite was like a tiger, cruel and wild.
As boars in combat once they're riled
That froth white as foam when in the flood,
Ankle-deep they fought in blood.
(*Enter THESEUS, HYPPOLITA and EMILY*)

THESEUS: Stop! How dare you fight in this unseemly way? You engage like men of birth and breeding and yet there is not present any judge or referee. Lay down your arms, on pain of death! Explain your actions without delay.

PALAMON: O Sir, we are both to blame, and both deserve to die. I am Palamon that has escaped; and this is Arcite that was set free and has deceived you as your servant. We are both in love with Emily.

EMILY: (*Surprised*) Oh!

PALAMON: I pray you, slay me in her sight – but Arcite too must die.

THESEUS: Your confession has been marked. Death is my decree.
(*HYPPOLITA and EMILY begin to cry*)

KNIGHT: And though by Theseus' anger they were accused.
By his noble reason they were both excused.

THESEUS: This seems to be your lucky day. Against my better judgement, my heart has been softened by the feminine touch. I suppose that, in your predicament, I would have acted much the same. You could have lived in freedom, yet you chose to risk your life for Emily. This, then, is what I decide. Go your ways, and in twelve months' time return hither to this ground. Bring with you each a hundred Knights prepared for tournament and I shall build the lists upon this spot. I will judge without grace or favour who shall prove the victor, and whoever it may be shall have the hand of Emily.

KNIGHT: Who looks ecstatic now but Palamon?

15

And who jumps for joy but Arcite?
They took their leave and homeward began to ride
to the walled city of Thebes, side by side.
The day approached when they should return,
each with a hundred Knights, armoured in readiness
for the fight of fights.
(PALAMON and ARCITE kneel in prayer)

PALAMON: O Venus. Venus. O Venus! Have pity on my pain and I shall
ever live in thy service. If I am to win the hand of Emily,
please give me a sign.

ARCITE: O Mars, God of War, I know that you, of all Gods,
understand the fire that burns within me. Please, I pray
you, help me in the fight tomorrow. I shall serve you till I
die. I beg of you a sign.

EMILY: (Kneels) O, Diana, Goddess of all virgins and the woodland
green, look on thy servant with mercy. I have followed your
ways all my life, being a virgin and a huntress. Let Palamon
and Arcite resolve their feud, and I will evermore be happy
to remain apart from men. But if that is not to be, then grant
that he who desires me most receives my prize. I pray you
give me a sign.

KNIGHT: Great was the festival in Athens, that day.
Dancing and singing, it being the lusty time of May,
Yeomen on foot, and commoners too
Armed with short sticks, and music they blew
On pipes, trumpets, clarions and drums
Like the sound of war as the enemy comes.
Many times they crossed in battle;
Each were victims of the sword's cruel rattle.
There shiver the shafts upon the shields so thick.
Through the breast-bone a warrior feels the prick;
Up spring the spears, twenty foot in height;
Out go the sword-blades, silver-bright.
Leather helmets they slash and shred,
Out gushes the blood so thick and red.
With mighty maces the bones are crushed,
One through the thickest throng is thrust.
Strong steeds stumble, and down goes all,
Rider underfoot, spinning like a ball.
This one parries with wild truncheon blows
As another brave warrior from his horse he throws.

(*PALAMON and ARCITE fight. PALAMON is injured and thrown from his horse*)

THESEUS: Enough! The deed is done. Fortune has decreed that Arcite is the winner. He shall have the hand of Emily.

KNIGHT: At this a thunderous clamour rent the air;
The fierce Arcite, his head held bare,
No helmet now, proud to show his face,
Riding full length of the trysting place,
Looking upwards to Emily on high,
And she at him with longing eye.
When suddenly, Arcite's horse ran wild
And leapt aside; and leaping, stumbled,
As from the saddle Arcite tumbled.
On the stone-hard ground he struck his head
And lay quite motionless, as if he were dead.
(*EMILY rushes to Arcite's side*)

ARCITE: Emily, O my Emily.

EMILY: I pledge myself to you. I trust the ways of Fortune. You are the victor of my love.

ARCITE: Emily, my love. If I should die in this my happiest hour, I bequeath my spirit to your service.

EMILY: My love, my noble prince, I pray you, do not leave me. Stay with me, my love.

ARCITE: My breath is not much more. Take me in your arms. I have suffered pain and anguish for your love and now I must die. Do not forget that Palamon has lived in torment, too. He will serve you well, if ever you should wish to take a husband. Farewell, my Emily. (*Dies*)

EMILY: Arcite! My love!

(*THESEUS, HYPPOLITA and PALAMON stand round the body of ARCITE in silence*)

KNIGHT: A sepulchre was built for Arcite, upon the spot where he had fought for the hand of Emily. The funeral ceremony was carried out at great expense, in royal splendour. Palamon returned to Thebes in sorrow. Emily wept day and

17

night in memory of her prince. A few years later Theseus summoned Palamon to Athens and persuaded Emily to feel pity for him. As was Arcite's wish they were married, and thereafter lived in happiness and health. So ends the story of Palamon and Arcite, and the means by which Fortune resolved their love for fair Emily.
(Cast take their bows)

M.C: Congratulations, everyone. Well done, Sir Andrew. Ladies and gentlemen, Sir Andrew Knight and the Knight's Tale.

MILLER: That was boring.

M.C: It was lyrical. Uplifting. Spiritually rewarding.

MILLER: I know. Boring.

M.C: Could we have the draw for the next tale?
(Draw is announced. While costumes are being changed Miller tells jokes. Refreshment break, if required.)

The Reeve's Tale

M.C:	The Reeve was choleric and fairly thin,
	His beard was shaved as near as ever he can.
	Long were his legs and very lean,
	Like knitting needles, there were no calfs to be seen.
	His ledgers were perfectly numbered and lettered,
	As an accountant he couldn't be bettered.
	Ladies and gentlemen, the Right Honourable Barry Reeve
	with the Reeve's tale.
REEVE:	First let me say without pretence
	The tale I tell bears no offence
	To anyone, assembled here, *(MILLER interrupts)*
	(Except for him who's full of beer)
	For by coincidence, upon my life,
	I tell of a Miller and his wife.
	Also his daughter, a tasty crumpet.
	By the way, this Miller played a trumpet.
	(MILLER produces trumpet and blows a few notes)
	Not very well.
	Now Simpkins was the Miller's name;
	A vile rogue, he poached all kind of game.
	Whenever folks brought corn to grind,
	He helped himself – he was that way inclined.
	He wore a Sheffield dagger in his hose,
	Round was his face and squashed was his nose.
	Curly as a coot he was. To speak more fully
	He was a thorough-going market-place bully.
	His wife however, it must be said,
	Was what genealogists call well bred.
	Her father was a priest, that's true,
	Though who her mother was, no one knew.
	She put on airs and affected style
	But woe if at her any man dared smile.
	For Simpkins was a jealous beast
	And capable of murder at the very least.
	And late in life they'd both been caught
	There was a six month baby as an afterthought.
	So let us now our tale unfold
	And if you find the action bold,
	Before you throw a cup or saucer
	Don't blame me, but Geoffrey Chaucer.
	Two students from a Cambridge College

19

Theology was their brand of knowledge.
(STUDENTS enter. They sing)

"O, Trinity Hall is the best
From North, South, East or West
As we pass by
You can hear men cry
Trinity Hall is the best."

REEVE: They'd bet each other that with tricks the same
They'd beat the Miller at his own game.

JOHN: I say, old chap, that Bible-class was boring
You woke me up with all your snoring.

ALAN: You're dashed well right, old chap, old John.
In fact I think we'll skip that don,
And take the corn to Simpkins' Mill,
We'll soon outwit him with our skill.

JOHN: Gosh, Alan, what a ripping wheeze!
We'll stop him cheating us with ease.

ALAN: I hear he's got a topping daughter,
I fancy a bit of what I didn't oughter.

JOHN: I say, Al, that's rather saucy.
Come on, we'd better load the horsey.
(Actor plays horse and wears straw hat with horses' ears. Halter round neck. Gives one of the students a piggy-back)

REEVE: And so they went, this Cambridge pair,
With corn sacks piled upon the mare.
The journey wasn't very long,
And as they went they sang a song.

"O, Trinity Hall is supreme,
As examples of men we're the cream.
It's not just a myth
That our wit has such pith
Yes, Trinity Hall is supreme."

(STUDENTS unload corn bags from the horse)

ALAN: Is there a nice young lady who'd like to hold my Dobbin for

a moment? Come on Dobbin.
*(Takes horse into audience. Asks someone to take his halter. Enter
MILLER, wheeling his grinding machine)*

JOHN: Good day, my man, we've brought our corn
But by tonight we must be gone,
So be a sport and do it quick.
You will? Oh, thanks, you are a brick.

MILLER: Anything to oblige students, that's my way;
So while I grind it, go away.
I mean, if it pleases you, kind sirs,
Go for a walk. I'll only be a couple of hours.

ALAN: Thanks all the same but I'm quite keen
To see you work your grinding machine.

JOHN: Me too, I'll watch the corn go down the spout.

ALAN: And I'll watch the bottom as the meal comes out.

MILLER: *(Aside)* That's what you think, you crafty pair,
You won't catch me out, so beware.
There's none to match my kind of fiddle
(to JOHN and ALAN) Just popping out, lads, for a jimmy
riddle.

REEVE: So round the back the Miller sidled
And the student's horse he soon unbridled.
(Releases horse from its minder. Tells it to clear off.)
Off like the clappers he went, over the gate;
Eagerly sniffing the air for a mate.
All afternoon fat Simpkins toiled,
The students unaware that they'd been foiled.
They watched him as the corn was ground,
Never daring to look around.

JOHN: The job is finished, there's been no robbin',
I'm just going out to look at Dobbin.

ALAN: Right-o, old sport, I'll hang on here.
I'll watch old Simpkins don't you fear.

REEVE: Soon the meal was bagged up tight
When in rushed John in quite a fright.

JOHN: Alan, quick, I think we're sunk,
                       Dobbin's gone and done a bunk.

REEVE: Off they shot like cork and stopper,
                       While Simpkins robbed them good and proper.
                       The Miller's daughter watched the fun
                       While Mrs. Simpkins fed her son.

MOLLY: Oh, mother, come quickly and see the boys prance!
                       Their horse is quite frenzied, they don't stand a chance.
                       Young Alan's gone down, O Lord, what a farce!
                       The horse stopped so quick he ran into its arse.
                       No, hang on. John's got it – he's just grabbed the mane
                       Ouch, it just kicked him – he won't walk again.
                       (STUDENTS and Dobbin chase round auditorium)

JOHN: Look out!

ALAN: Behind you now!

JOHN: Whoa, there old Dob.

ALAN: You've missed him.

JOHN: It's your fault.

ALAN: O shut your gob.

MOLLY: They're off again running, Alan's trousers are down.
                       John's caught up a tree by the sleeves of his gown,
                       Who'd ever believe it? – they've caught him at last,
                       I never knew students could run quite so fast.
                       They surely must be bruised and battered;
                       In fact they look completely knackered.

MILLER: Now then lads, enjoy the chase?
                       You've got horse muck on your face,
                       You've lost the trousers off your bum.
                       You won't half cop it from your Mum.

JOHN: Come on, let's take the corn and go.
                       You take this and I'll – Oh no!

MILLER: What's up, lads?

ALAN: Well where's our corn?

MILLER: You don't mean to tell me some of it's gone?
Times are bad, all this rape and pillage,
There's a rough lot live in this 'ere village.

ALAN: We've caught the nag, but lost the grain,
The Miller's done us yet again.
It's too late now to set off back
We'll have to stay the night, dear Jack.

JOHN: It's dashed bad luck we're in this plight,
Do you think there's a chance of a room for the night?

MILLER: A room? I'm afraid I haven't any. *(Opens his hand)*
Oh, what's this, I see, a penny? *(more money)*

JOHN: Some food?

MILLER: Perhaps.

ALAN: A drink? *(more money)*

MILLER: Could be.

BOTH: How much?

MILLER: It'll cost a pretty p... *(Gives him bagful of money)*
On second thoughts I hate animosity,
Where would we be without generosity? Come in, lads.

REEVE: Down Simpkins' gullet the cold beer gushed,
And even his wife was pretty flushed.
Into the night they sang a rousing chorus,
To sing it here would be to bore us.

ALL: Rubbish. *(etc.)*
(Ad lib Miller: "Let's have a mucky song" etc., "Who knows a mucky song?" etc.)

MILLER: *(Sings)* "Oh the cow kicked Nelly in the belly in the barn

And the farmer said it wouldn't do her any harm."

MOLLY: *(Sings)* "I'll sing you a song about a young farmer Dick,

Who was curly and cuddly and careful and quick.
He loved making hay when the bright sun did shine,
First he'd toss his hay, then he'd toss mine.
He tossed it all once, he tossed it all twice,
He tossed it all three times because it was nice.

He'd handle my sheaves and he'd pile up the rick,
His pitchfork was sharp and his bales were so thick.
We'd bundle it backwards and stack it up tight,
We'd make hay together all through the night.
We'd turn over once, we'd turn over twice,
We'd turn over three times because it was nice.

But now he's away and there's no more Dick,
And I'm left alone with a rain-sodden rick.
So all you young maids who are both foolish and free,
Don't make the mistake and make hay like me.
For I've little boy once, I've little boy twice,
I've little boy three times because it was nice."

STUDENTS: *(Sing)* "Oh, Trinity Hall is the best.
From North, South, East or West..."

MILLER: Oh, no – not that one again. You've sung that ten times already. Let the missus sing one. Come on, love, give us a religious one. Down on your knees, everyone. Let's have a bit of religion.
(One of the students accompanies her on organ, harmonium or whatever instrument is being used. She sings song very straight.)

MRS. SIMPKINS: *(Sings)* "I pray the Lord to keep me safe,
To keep me warm and snug.
And every night I'm wrapped up tight,
Snug as a bug in a rug."

ALL: "Oh Lord"

MRS. SIMPKINS: "Snug as a bug in a rug"

ALL: "Yea yea"

MRS. SIMPKINS: "Snug as a bug in a rug"

ALL: "Right on."

REEVE: At last worn out, it was time to rest,
          Where would they all sleep? Ah, you guessed.

ALAN: Which is our room?

REEVE: Young Alan said.

MILLER: In here with us. That's the bed
          It's big enough to take us all.
          She's on the left, we're in the middle, you're by the wall.
          *(The bed is suggested by two blankets or sheets stitched together
          on a rope, held at one side by the REEVE, and at the other by
          DOBBIN at shoulder height so that we just see the heads of the
          actors when they are behind it.)*

REEVE: Forthwith the five-some did retire
          And soon the Miller he expired.
          Then his wife began to snooze,
          Of course, they'd had a lot of booze.
          The girl soon joined the land of Nod.
          (She was sleeping on her tod)
          No need to worry about the tiny tot,
          He was tucked up in his cot.
          *(The baby is in a small wooden box on the floor in front of the
          Miller's wife)*
          But John and Alan lay awake,
          The Miller's snores made such a quake.

ALAN: I'll get my own back on that ass,
          I'm going to jump upon his lass.

JOHN: Careful, Alan, stealthy as a stoat,
          If he wakes up he'll cut your throat.

ALAN: He'll never wake, he's quite pie-eyed.
          I'll wager she's a damn good ride.

REEVE: So out of bed bold Alan crept
          And soon upon the maid he leapt.
          The Miller never heard the thump
          As the lusty pair began to jump.
          By the time that they'd abated
          Poor Old John was quite frustrated.

JOHN: A joke's a joke, but this is ridiculous.

I feel a right fool, while they're both knickerless.
My pal's got his own back for the wrong that was done,
He's having a great time, giving her one.
I'll look a real twerp when this story gets out,
They'll say I'm a weed and a booby, no doubt.

REEVE: Just then the bedroom door did squeak,
As the Miller's wife went for a leak.
(Exit Miller's wife)

JOHN: I've watched my chum enjoy his play,
It's my turn now to have my end away.
I'll put the cot beside my bed,
And she'll get in with me instead.

MRS. SIMPKINS: *(Enters)* Where am I? It's dark as pitch,
I don't know which bed is which.
Where's the cot? I left it here;
If I got in with the boys – oh dear!
Ah, here it is I've found the cot.
(Gets into bed with John)
In bed at last; what's this that's hot?

REEVE: The Miller's wife then lay quite still
And soon her senses felt a thrill.
She thought her husband had been asleep,
So she was pleased when he thrust deep.
All through the night the couples lusted
Until the bedsprings were nearly busted.
(Anvil chorus. Heads, feet etc. appear in various permutations. Miller asleep throughout.

ALAN: Oh, Molly dear, it'll soon be light.
You were jolly good, d'you feel alright?

MOLLY: Oh yes thanks, Alan. I've learned a lot,
I'd like some more, but we'd better not.
Oh, by the way, the corn my father thieved
'S behind the door, don't forget it, he'll be right peeved.

ALAN: Thanks Molly for what you've said,

Now I'll get back to my own bed.
Oops, there's the cot, beside your Mother,
Our bed must be the other.

(Gets into bed with the MILLER)
Wake up you dolt, and don't dare scoff,
Three times with Molly I've had it off!
I'll tell our chums that you were snoring
While I spent the whole night whoring.

MILLER: What's that you said, you dirty skunk?
You've been up Molly while I was drunk?
I'll murder you for that, you swine!
I'll have your guts for a washing line.
(MILLER goes for ALAN. ALAN hits him on the nose)

REEVE: Alan was caught by his Adam's apple,
While their fists were flailing in a furious battle.
Then he punched the Miller's snout,
All down his nightshirt the blood poured out.

MRS. SIMPKINS: Wake up, husband, those boys are fighting!
What a night – it's been quite exciting.

REEVE: She could just see the shapes of the battling two
Not clearly enough to know who was who,
And meaning to give Alan a blow to the head
It was the Miller's curly skull received it instead,
And down he went, crying

MILLER: I'm going to die!

REEVE: So they just put the boot in, and there let him lie.

ALAN: Farewell, dear Moll, I enjoyed our frolicking
But I'm afraid your Dad deserved that rollicking.

JOHN: I say Mrs. S. you really were lusty
It was me that oiled where you were rusty.

REEVE: And so our tale comes to an end
In hope that the Miller's ways will mend;
And if you think that bits were dirty
I beg you, please, don't get shirty,
For in our story a moral's hid –
'Do and be done by as you did.'
(The draw is made for the next tale. Since it will be short, an interval at this point is not recommended. As soon as the singers are ready the M.C. introduces the Cook's Tale.)

The Cook's Tale

M.C:

A Cook they had with them, for the nonce,
To boil the chickens with the marrow bones.
He could roast, seethe, boil and fry,
Make a good stew or bake a pie,
Unfortunately, it seemed a great pity
That he had gangrene on his knee;
An open sore, yellow with pus;
His blancmange and custard was delicious.

(Sung)

"We'll sing you a tale, its moral is clear,
About a young prentice as you will now hear.
He'd black curly hair and a countenance brown,
The lasses took care as he jigged up and down.
Up away, hey away, he's no good
As gay as a goldfinch in the wood.

CHORUS *(Sung as a round)*
Dance a jig and jump for joy.
Pretty Peterkin he's the boy,
With the wenches he's a devil,
Take them Peterkin in your revel.
Young Peter he served in the victualling trade,
But he gambled much more than he ever was paid.
From work he played truant, his life was a game,
And his master rebuked him again and again.
Up away, he away, how they sang
Revelling Peterkin and his gang.

CHORUS

He hadn't a rival in throwing the dice,
There was none could compete when it came to vice.
He'd drink and he'd dance, never missing a jig,
And all the girls loved him, little or big.
Up away, hey away, can't keep still
Peterkin's fingers in the till.

CHORUS

His master sat down and he started to think,
His other apprentices would fall to the drink.
If one rotten apple you find in the store,

Throw it away in case it rots more.
Up away, hey away, don't come back
Poor old Peterkin's got the sack."

END OF ACT ONE

(Refreshments, songs, and general merriment)

(M.C. restores order, restrains MILLER, and gives notice of recommencement of performance. Draw for next tale.)

The Wife of Bath's Tale

M.C:
There was a worthy wife from Bath in Somerset.
A bit deaf unfortunately, but far from dumb as yet.
Her stockings were scarlet, her shoes were new.
Bold and comely was her face, red in hue;
An excellent woman all her life.
As for husbands she'd gone through five.
(Apart from other men in her early life,)
But we won't talk of that. This good wife
Knew all the remedies of love, perchance,
For in that art she knew every dance.

WIFE:
My tale takes place in days of yore,
When fairies ruled from shore to shore.
Elves and sprites of many kinds
Made mockery of people's minds.
Once there was, in days gone by
A handsome knight with roving eye,
(Enter MILLER Knight, playing it straight)
Whilst walking in the summer's air,
Beheld a maiden, very fair.
He tempted her with words of chivalry
But she resolved to save her chastity.
She fought and strove to save her treasure
But soon by force he took his pleasure.
And thus the poor girl's flower was plucked,
(This scene we dare not reconstruct.)
Throughout the land there came a cry

CHORUS:
"To rape is wrong, this Knight must die."

WIFE:
To court he came to stand his trial
For failing to exercise self-denial.

KING:
I condemn outright your vile misdeed,
It's against the law to scatter seed;
Where pure young maidens are involved.
I've considered well and have resolved,
Taking account of the poor girl's shock,
That you should die upon the block.

QUEEN:	O, husband dear, I beg a favour, Let me be judge of his behaviour. I will not take an indulgent stance But let him earn his second chance.
KING:	Very well, my sweet, my duck. It's up to you, the best of luck.
QUEEN:	I am not offering absolution Unless you give the right solution. This is the question to be diagnosed "What do women desire most?" Answer if it's on your tongue But if you're wrong your days are done, So listen well to what I say. You may go free for one year and a day. But then you must return to court With the answer you have sought.
KNIGHT:	I thank you for the year's reprieve, What the answer is I can't conceive. And so I will be on my way To seek the truth, without delay.
WIFE:	*(Sings)* "He searched and searched in vain Sun, moon, stars, rain. Night and day, wind and tide, Tree and leaf, summer sighed. Autumn wept, winter slept, Spring awoke in pain. He asked and asked in vain." *(Enter WOMAN 1 in drag)*
KNIGHT:	Can I ask you something?
WOMAN 1:	Yes, what is it?
KNIGHT:	Excuse me, madam.
WOMAN 1:	Miss.
KNIGHT:	I beg your pardon. What do you want most?
WOMAN 1:	Ooh you naughty man – come here!

MILLER: Get off!
(Enter WOMAN 2 in drag)

KNIGHT: Hullo.

WOMAN 2: Hullo, soldier.

KNIGHT: Can I ask you something? What do you desire most?

WOMAN 2: Guess.

KNIGHT: It's very hard.

WOMAN 2: You're getting warm.

KNIGHT: Lots of clothes.

WOMAN 2: You're cold again.
(Enter WOMAN 3 in drag)

WOMAN 3: Who's this looking butch and hairy?
I hope it's the new man from the dairy.
Two large yoghurts please.

KNIGHT: Please let me make my story clear,
I've asked this question for a year.
Tomorrow I return to court
And if I'm wrong my life's cut short.
Please help me, what do you suggest?
(The WOMEN huddle together in consultation)

WOMAN 1: Well, I don't know really.

WIFE: Some said, women desire

WOMAN 2: Lots of money.

WIFE: Some said

WOMAN 3: Honour.

WIFE: One said

WOMAN 1: Well, that's funny, I like new clothes.

WOMAN 2:	And lust in bed.
WOMAN 3:	To be widowed often. And then re-wed.
WIFE:	Some said
WOMAN 1:	The best way to win our hearts is with flattery. That's what pleases our private parts.
WIFE:	And I'd agree, the man who flatters is the one who gives pleasure where it matters.
KNIGHT:	I'm none the wiser, as you see No two women can agree. Thanks all the same, I mean no rebuff, But I'm afraid it's just not good enough.
WOMAN 2:	Well, you're a nice one, that's for sure!
WOMAN 1:	You won't get no help from me no more. *(WOMEN exit)*
KNIGHT:	I must return to face the Queen And death for this said libertine. Why did I steal that maiden's goods? It's never worth it afterwards. But lo! I've just seen something cheering. Two dozen ladies in that clearing, They're performing an amazing dance. I'll pop my question. It's my last chance. Hello, what's happened? Just as I spoke They vanished – went up in smoke. There's no one, save an ugly hag, She's coming closer – what a bag! *(Enter HAG, i.e. actress wearing mask)*
HAG:	Young man, I am here to help you out, I'm old enough to know what life's about.
KNIGHT:	Dear mother, come what may, I am dead if I can't say What it is that women most desire. If you could enlighten me, I'll pay your hire.
HAG:	You must promise, give me your hand,

I'll make a request very soon, and
You must do it, if it's within your might.
I'll answer your question before tonight.

KNIGHT: Here's my hand. I agree to that.

HAG: In that case, I'll eat my hat
If you're not saved, cross my heart and hope to die,
The Queen will say the same as I.

WIFE: This compact sealed, then off they sped
Towards the court to save his head.
The hag and the Knight arrived at court,
And he said to the Queen…

KNIGHT: I've kept my word, and here I am;
and this is the answer if it please you, Ma'am.

QUEEN: I'm glad to see you've kept your date,
Give the answer, then you'll know your fate.

KNIGHT: The answer is this, Your Majesty,
All a woman wants is sovereignty,
To rule husband, lover, home and heart;
Queen and mistress from the start.

WIFE: In all the court everyone was agreed
The Knight had saved his life indeed.

QUEEN: That's it! Now female hearts will all awake;
No more maids by force you'll take.

HAG: Excuse me, ma'am, before you go,
I think there's something you ought to know.
I gave the answer to this Knight
On condition that he saw me right.
We're all agreed I've saved his life,
Now he must take me for his wife.

KNIGHT: Surely this is fun you're poking,
Marry you! You must be joking!
I know I said I'd grant your wish,
But you're not exactly a tasty dish.
Think again, ask me another,
You're old enough to be my mother.

QUEEN:	If this be true and you gave your oath, Then you must surely plight your troth.
COURTIERS:	Quite right.
HAG:	It's thanks to me that you're not dead, Now take me to the nuptial bed.
KNIGHT:	No chance. *(The KNIGHT escapes, and is pursued and caught by the COURTIERS who restrain him as he is wed. They then force him into bed with the HAG.)*
WIFE:	And in the end the Knight submitted, For soon in wedlock they were knitted. Out of the fat into the fire, he thought, As he and his wife to their bed were brought. He wallowed about and he tossed and he turned, While his wife was waiting for the pleasure she'd earned.
HAG:	Come, dear husband, hold me tight, This is a poor do on our wedding night. We should be having healthy fun, What's the matter? What've I done?
KNIGHT:	It's not that you've committed sin, It's what you are; a hag with a hairy chin. You're common, old, ugly, poor; You're an old boot – d'you want any more?
HAG:	Well this is charming, on our wedding night, I think you could be a bit more polite. You just said I was foul and old Well, you certainly won't be made a cuckold, For filth and age are certainly Wonderful guardians of chastity. Nevertheless, since I know your delights, I'll look after your worldly appetites. I'll give you two choices, by and by; To have me smelly and old till I die And be to you a true and humble wife And never displease you all my life; Or else you can have me young and fair And take your chance with those who dare To come into your house because of me,

(And quite likely in other places, maybe.)
I can arrange a transformation,
I'll be young and pretty – a decoration,
But I can't promise to be true.
Now take your choice, it's up to you.

WIFE: Indecision span round his head
        Until at last he sighed and said...

KNIGHT: I want what's best for both of us.
        You choose, love, I want no fuss.

HAG: You've given me the mastery, then?

KNIGHT: Yes, I couldn't go through all that again.

HAG: You'll be better off than other fellahs
        Whose faithless wives are bodysellers.
        As my magic spell unfurls
        You'll have the very best of both worlds;
        Young and faithful, you'll live to thank it.
        I'll just get changed beneath the blanket.

WIFE: The hag then vanished out of sight
        And reappeared all bathed in light.
        (Reappears without mask. Romantic music etc.)
        And so they lived to their life's end
        In perfect joy. May Christ please send
        Husbands, young, meek and fresh in bed,
        And grace to override the ones we wed.
        For those who lead the happiest lives
        Are husbands governed by their wives.

The Franklyn's Tale

M.C:
A Franklyn was in the company,
His beard was as white as a daisy,
His complexion it was sanguine,
He was partial to wine in the early morning.
At the county sessions he was Lord and Sire
And he had been elected for the Shire.
A dagger and a purse made of silk
Hung from his girdle, white as milk.
Sheriff and auditor he'd been and yet
He was the finest example of the county set.
(All the Franklyn's lines are sung, operatically.)

FRANKLYN:
In Brittany there lived in honour bound
A Knight unto a lady that he'd found.
This noble couple were in such accord
She took him for her husband and her lord.

ARVERAGUS:
Sweet Dorigen I promise as a Knight
Ever to obey you as a servant might.
Not strict or jealous will this husband be.
And in name alone have mastery.

DORIGEN:
Arveragus, my love you'll never lose.
This gift of freedom I'll not abuse,
But be always faithful and cause no strife
Sir, I am your true and humble wife.

FRANKLYN:
So as man and wife in blissful joy they dwelt,
By Finisterre's coast, till the fair lord felt
In Britain he must his fortunes swell
By deeds of arms. Dorigen farewell.
(They embrace and part)

DORIGEN:
Each day is as eternity
That we are parted by the sea,
O blessed Lord, that sits above
I pray you, guard my own sweet love
And when he does return to port
Let him not upon the rocks be caught.
Those fiendish rocks that haunt my every day,
Those crags where many ships are led astray.
The fear that in my heart does dwell

Pleads that those rocks be sunk in hell.
(Enter LADY)

LADY: Dear Lady, why this sombre attitude?
Every day you spend in solitude.
I beg you let me ease your sorrow,
Join our party on the morrow.
Your husband's gone, I won't deny it
But have some fun, why don't you try it?

FRANKLYN: So Dorigen at last relented
And with misgivings she consented.
Next day saw her at the dance,
She gave no man a second glance.
For faithful she would ever be
And always walk in constancy.
(Dance)
Now at the dance there was a squire
Who truth to tell did much admire
Fair Dorigen. For two long years
He'd bottled up his hopes and fears.
Aurelius was his name, young and lusty,
Consumed with love, but very trusty.
At length, on finding them alone
He confessed his love, to her unknown.

AURELIUS: Madam, I beg you for some small sign
That you may return my love in time.

DORIGEN: Aurelius, I am determined all my life
To stay an ever faithful wife.

AURELIUS: By the stars in heaven and the moon above
Is there nothing I can do to prove my love?
I fear that I will surely die
And so my love, to life goodbye.

DORIGEN: I can only promise what you ask
If you perform an impossible task.
Remove each rock along the shore,
And I will love you evermore.

AURELIUS: But truly that's beyond man's scope.
Is there no other way to give me hope?

DORIGEN: Aurelius, my dear good friend
             I'll love my husband to the end.
             So please, I humbly beg of you
             Invest your love in someone new.
             (Exit)

AURELIUS: Fair Dorigen, my love, my life,
             Why was I stricken by another's wife?
             To move those rocks is quite impossible,
             Even to attempt it is unimaginable.
             And so I am resolved to die,
             Oh, help me please you gods on high.

FRANKLYN: With that the poor man lost his sense
             And to his bed was taken thence.
             His brother sought to find a cure
             But nothing helped this unloved wooer.
             His emotion drove him to distraction
             Until his brother forced some action.
             Together they travelled far and wide,
             Seeking help on every side.
             At last they came across a mystic
             Very supernaturalistic.
             Of him they asked some special magic
             To help prevent a fate most tragic.
             (Enter GURU. Guru music)

GURU: Come in, my sons. By my deduction
             You've come for lessons and instruction.
             I have a course, it starts next week;
             Twenty pounds an hour, that's very cheap.

BROTHER: As a matter of fact, we need some tricks,
             My brother he is in a fix.

GURU: Fix?

BROTHER: He'll pay you well to move some rocks.

GURU: Some rocks you say, now let me see,
             A one-off job? A thousand quid's my fee.

BROTHER: A thousand pounds, that's very steep.

GURU: You want me to do it on the cheap?

BROTHER: A thousand then, the bargain make,
I cannot risk a slight mistake.

GURU: I think you'll be well satisfied,
Now I must study moon and tide.
So watch the tides with guile and stealth
And leave the details to myself.
(Delves in bag for magic ingredients)
Now I am eating a mystic potion,
Jellied eels from the Indian Ocean.
Bombay duck and Delhi mutton,
Black bits from my belly button.
Bhuna prawn and wombat's winkle,
On my cymbal I am having a tinkle.
Abracadabra from here to Darjeeling –
Give those rocks a sinking feeling!

FRANKLYN: And as the mystic had thus spoken,
The logic of the waves was broken.
And for a week the rocks were hidden,
Aurelius had done what he was bidden,
For now the rocks were out of sight.

ALL: *(Sing)* O pity
Dorigen's awful plight.

AURELIUS: My sovereign lady. I've done all that you bade.
I love you; remember the pact that we made.
Under the cliffs no rocks can be found
And therefore it's to me you'll always be bound.

DORIGEN: If I had thought that you'd succeed,
To love you I'd not have agreed.
This pledge has caused me untold sorrow,
I'll give my answer on the morrow.

FRANKLYN: So sadly Dorigen weighed her plight,
Death or dishonour, which was right?
Between the two she could not decide
And on her knees she prayed and cried.
Now Arveragus, who homeward nears,
Sees his wife and observes her tears.
No longer can the truth be veiled
And soon he knows what is entailed.

ARVERAGUS: O death, despair, O darkest hour!
The blossom has blown before the flower.
Honour and truth hold sway in life
And so farewell, my love, my wife.

FRANKLYN: When Aurelius received her word
And saw the sorrow that in her stirred,
He marvelled at her husband's will
And guilt within his heart did fill.

AURELIUS: Madam. Say to your Lord, Arveragus
That since I recognise his nobleness
To you, and seeing your distress
That he prefers the shame and taints incurred,
Than with me you should break your word;
I myself would rather suffer pain
Than ever hurt you and your Lord again.
From our bond I now release you
And will depart, so may it please you,
Knowing you the best and truest wife
That ever yet I knew in all my life.

FRANKLYN: Now then, ladies, tell me true
Which seemed the noblest act to you,
Aurelius, Arveragus or his wife?
Who owed the greatest debt to life?

The Nun's Priest's Tale

NARRATOR: Here's a tale of tragedy and fun
That takes place long ago in a chicken-run,
Beside the cottage of a widow named Gwen,
Who lived with her daughter, some pigs and a hen
Or two; these hens, I should say, were her pride and joy;
Seven all told, plus a cock, quite a boy.
Chanticleer his name, listen to him crow.
(CHANTICLEER enters and crows)
Most of the day he's on the go.
Smart in appearance, and doesn't he know it
As round the yard he'll step and toe it.
(CHANTICLEER parades himself)
Red is his comb, like a fire it glows.
Blue are his legs and red are his toes.
He knows it all, this golden charm-cock,
At telling the time, he's like an alarm clock.
Quite a one with the ladies too,
He served them well to give him his due.
But the special favourite that claimed his vote
Was a Rhode Island redhead, called Pertelote.
A pretty chick with a dimpled face,
She knew all the ways of social grace.
She walked like a Queen, and sang like a linnet;
If there was a prize for charm, she'd surely win it.
And every night on the perch she used ter
Sit next to her beloved rooster.
(CHANTICLEER and PERTELOTE balance on perch)
Alas, for fear of toppling, their sport was inhibited,
So, to a peck on the cheek, their good-night was limited.
One night, Pertelote was kept awake
By Chanticleer making the bed-post shake.
She'd never seen him in this state before
Groaning, screeching, afflicted sore.

PERTELOTE: Are you alright? You seem distressed,
You haven't had a good night's rest.
Chanticleer, dearest, turn it in,
Since half past three you've made that din.
I've hardly had a wink of sleep,
I'm sick and tired of counting sheep.

CHANTICLEER: What a night! I've had a right scare,

I think it might have been a nightmare.
But it seemed that real I nearly died,
I'm so relieved to be here by your side.

PERTELOTE: Scared of dreams? You silly coot.

CHANTICLEER: I was being chased, dear, by an ugly great brute.

PERTELOTE: A dream's a dream and nothing more,
There's no excuse for that uproar.

CHANTICLEER: There's dreams and dreams, I'll have you know;
If you'd seen the beast I'm sure you'd crow.
A bit like a dog with reddish tint
And beady eyes with a fiery glint,
A bushy tail and a pointed snout.
It could've turned me inside out.

PERTELOTE: I'm ashamed of you, you cowardly bird
That's quite the feeblest thing I've heard.

CHANTICLEER: And what about Pharaoh in the Bible?
And other people more reliable.
They've awoken in the morning
And found their dream a truthful warning.
So I'd be grateful if you didn't mock,
It won't be so funny when I'm a dead cock.

PERTELOTE: The cause of dreams is without question
Nothing more than indigestion.
And therefore Chanticleer, I urge
You quickly take a remedial purge.
You've had a bad night – all it means
You've eaten cabbage, or baked beans.
Here's a recipe for a laxative diet,
I'll give you the ingredients and you just try it.
Half a dozen worms big and fat.
Swallowed down with intestines of rat.
Twenty slugs and thirteen snails,
Two dozen maggots and four mouses' tails.

CHANTICLEER: Thanks very much but I've changed my mind.
My troubles, I think, are of another kind.
It's not a laxative I need,
I'll soon recover with some chicken-feed.

And your sweet presence by my side
Will help restore my injured pride.
Me, afraid of dreams? Heavens, what a jest!
Look at the sun, six o'clock, and we're not dressed.

NARRATOR: With that Chanticleer crowed a throaty reveille,
Which echoed around the yard and the valley.
Preening his feathers and airing his comb,
He strutted around his farmyard home.
Protected from harm by a fence of strong wire,
He paraded himself for all to admire.

CHANTICLEER: *(Sings)* "O, what a beautiful morning,
O, what a beautiful day!
I've got a wonderful feeling
Everything's coming my way."

NARRATOR: Soon the memory of his dream was gone
As he burst into melodious song.
(CHANTICLEER sings Elvis Presley song. PERTELOTE and hens swoon in admiration)
Completely enwrapped by the applause he received
The arrival of a fox went unperceived.
(CHANTICLEER continues singing, eventually notices the fox, and tries to retreat)

FOX: Don't go away my feathery friend,
I'd hate for that beautiful song to end.
I shouldn't be here, forgive my intrusion;
I was hypnotized by your elocution.
The style of your singing, you might like to know
Reminds me of how your papa used to crow.
A hero of mine, a dear friend as well,
Your father's sweet voice was clear as a bell.
The same intonation, the line of the neck,
He sang with his eyes closed, without hindrance or check.
So please, carry on, there's nothing to fear,
My intentions are musical, that's why I'm here.

NARRATOR: Quite unaware of the danger involved,
Chanticleer's caution was quickly dissolved.
He didn't know that foxes liked chicken
For the simple reason they were finger-lickin'.
And so he performed with his every ounce,
While the fox awaited the moment to pounce.

(*CHANTICLEER sings, exaggerating his performance, until he is singing with his eyes closed; as if in a trance. The fox grabs him by the neck. PERTELOTE and the other hens raise the alarm. GWEN, played as a pantomime dame, rushes out with a club in her hand*)

GWEN: You birds won't half get a packet,
What's the meaning of all this racket?
Cor blimey, bloomin' 'eck!
Chanticleer's got it in the neck.
I'll have that fox upon the block,
He's not having my lovely cock.
After him girls!
(*General chase*)

NARRATOR: Off ran the fox, the prize in his jaws,
As old mother Gwen, jumped into her drawers.
Her daughter gave chase, and Pertelote too,
You never heard such a hullaballoo.
Twice round the yard, twenty feet square,
Feathers flying everywhere.
Gwen was down upon her luck,
Skidding on some chicken muck.
Her daughter blew on a horn of brass
While poor old mum was on her arse.
Up she gets in the frantic mellee,
Down again upon her belly.
Alas, too late, the fox had fled,
And Chanticleer was as good as dead.
Gwen was forced to cease her chase,
The fox had reached his hiding place.
(*Exit GWEN, PERTELOTE etc. weeping and clucking*)
No hope for him that once crowed loud
No more to hold his head up proud.
Between the fox's teeth impaled
Our hero's coffin is surely nailed.
Observe now, friends, a change of luck
With Chanticleer's last impassioned cluck.

CHANTICLEER: Alright, Foxy, you've reached the thicket,
It looks like I'm on a sticky wicket.
Call off the chase, tell them I'm yours,
Tell them you've got me between your jaws.

FOX: A good idea!

NARRATOR: The fox replied.
Too late his mistake he realised,
As Chanticleer flew onto a bough.

CHANTICLEER: Ha, ha, clever dick, can't get me now.

FOX: Chanticleer, dearest friend, I apologise.
I can see I've upset you, from your eyes.
You misunderstand me, I'm no sinner,
It was a way of inviting you home for dinner.

CHANTICLEER: Thanks, but I'm not keen on that venue,
Besides I think I know who's on the menu.
You won't catch me a second time.
Bad luck, isn't it, foxes can't climb?

NARRATOR: And so the fox returned to his lair,
He'd learnt his lesson from this affair.
Keep your mind upon the job.

FOX: And if in doubt don't open your gob.

NARRATOR: Chanticleer, too, his lesson learned.
Never let your head be turned
By flattery. Nor close your eyes for affectation.

CHANTICLEER: Unless you fancy mutilation.

NARRATOR: Should you think this tale's untrue,
Dreaming chickens and talking foxes,
Remember, what happens to stuck-up cocks is,
Just as likely to happen to you.

The Pardoner's Tale

(TOM, DICK and HARRY, with BARMAID in pub.)

NARRATOR: Tom, Dick and Harry were three strong lads,
Drinking, gambling, lecherous cads.
In the pub from morn till night
They swilled their guts till they were tight.
And in between the glass and tap
They played high stakes for seven card snap.
They put the wenches through the hoop,
They'd never heard of brewer's droop.
Alas, one day, their manic quaffing,
Was interrupted by a passing coffin.
(Funeral bell. Coffin passes in silhouette)

TOM: Who's that, mine hostess? We want to know.

DICK: These pub-shows have hit an all-time low.

HARRY: We want some fun, as you know well,
There's nothing funny about that there bell.

BARMAID: That, fine lads, was Walter Scroggs.
A mate of yours, he's popped his clogs.
He was killed last night by a violent crime,
On his way home at closing time.

HARRY: Our old mate Walt? Why, that's a sin;
I'll get the bugger that did him in.
He'll not live long that is to blame
Once I find out his cursed name.

BARMAID: His name is Death, his victims many,
Corpses now are two a penny.
The plague is rife, the doctors say,
The gravedigger's on a twelve hour day.

DICK: Death, did you say? He won't live long,
I'll soon cut short his merry song.

TOM: So will we all, as here we stand
We'll call ourselves "The Avenging Band".
We'll swear an oath for Walter's sake,

And with this knife a pact we'll make.

NARRATOR: On saying thus they cut their wrists
And each the other's blood soon kissed.
And though from drink they were still sotted,
They upped and went before it clotted.
Before they'd walked a mile or so
They reached a place where willows grow,
And there they met an ancient crow,
Wrapped in flannel from head to toe.
She seemed a stranger to the place,
Well on in years, to judge by her face.

OLD LADY: Good day, young men, I wish you well.

HARRY: Don't be cheeky, rat bag.

TOM: Go to Hell.

HARRY: Don't you think it's time you were dead.

OLD LADY: Indeed I do, I'm past my prime,
After seventy it's an uphill climb.
My sinews now are withered rope,
To wait for death is my only hope.

DICK: Did you hear that, Tom? She waits for Death!
That's what she said with her stinking breath.

TOM: Death, did you say? – d'you know where he is?
Where can we find him? – we're friends of his.

HARRY: Come on, old hag, don't muck us about.
See my fist and feel the clout.

OLD LADY: It's Death you're after? I know his lair,
Follow my directions and you'll find him there.
Over the hedge and up the lane.
Turn right, then left, then right again.
Past the May tree, keep on straight
Till you reach a five-barred gate.
Then you'll see an oak tree tall,
And Death beside a dry-stone wall.

HARRY: We'll let you off, if that's no lie.

We hate to see old people die.

DICK: Come on, Harry, it's not her fault,
We're after the one that did for Walt.

TOM: The Avenging Band! Remember our pledge?
Come on let's find him, there's the hedge.

NARRATOR: The three then started on their way
Leaving the lady to live another day.
Up the lane, full half a mile,
Scouring the landscape all the while,
Past hedge and bush, through darkened glade,
Eager to fulfil the pact they'd made.
And soon they came upon the tree
Where they'd been told that Death would be.

HARRY: There's no one here, my two dear muckers.
She must think we're stupid suckers.

TOM: I can't believe it; she seemed so straight.
Perhaps we'd better sit and wait.

DICK: No chance, lads, I knew we'd cock it,
Hello, someone's got a hole in their pocket.
Look what's here, a heap of treasure,
We're rich, I tell you beyond all measure.

TOM: Gold and Silver, a thousand pound!
This must be Death's hoarding ground.

HARRY: We'll take the gold and split it thrice,
Lightning never strikes the same place twice.

DICK: Let's be off, before we're copped.
If we're seen with this we'll be surely stopped.

TOM: You're right, Dick, this stuff's a bit too hot,
They'll think we're robbers, and we'll be shot.

HARRY: The answer's simple; we'll stop right here
And when it's dark we'll homeward steer.

DICK: Stop here all day, without a drink?
Very funny Harry; I don't think.

TOM: To draw by lots would be most wise
       To see which one goes back for supplies.

NARRATOR: Without more fuss Tom found three sticks,
            They each drew one, the choice was Dick's.

DICK: Right lads, I won't be long,
        If you keep guard we can't go wrong.

TOM: Tara Dick, Keep your mouth shut tight,
       We won't be safe till it's dark tonight.

NARRATOR: Off toward the town he sped
            To fetch his mates some drink and bread.
            While Harry planned deeds vile and bold
            To deprive Dick of his life and his gold.
            "Why split the gold three ways?" he said
            "We could take half each, if Dick were dead."

HARRY: I have a scheme that cannot lose,
         We'll contrive a fight when he brings the booze.
         Pretend to wrestle with our friend Dick
         And in his back this blade I'll stick.
         We'll dig his grave beneath this tree,
         And back in the tavern we soon will be.

NARRATOR: They both agreed the evil plan
            And sat and waited for their man.
            But Dick had plans as well he might,
            His character being far from white.

DICK: Why split three ways?

NARRATOR: He also thought.

DICK: With all that gold, I'd not go short!

NARRATOR: So he paid a visit to a general grocer
            To buy a drug that makes death come closer.
            (DICK goes into shop, rings bell)

DICK: Shop! Come on, I haven't got all day
        Is anyone there? Hurry up, I say.
        (SHOPKEEPER/BARMAID appears)

SHOPKEEPER: Keep your hair on, you hasty man,
                 Barging in here like Desperate Dan.
                 This is a shop, not a barricade,
                 I don't have to serve you, I'm not short of trade.

DICK: You'll soon understand when you hear of my trouble.
                 The mice are eating my corn to stubble,
                 There's a rat up my drainpipe, a fox on the prowl,
                 My crops will be ruined and so will my fowl.
                 There's weeds on the paths and slugs in the ditches,
                 And not only that, there's ants in my breeches.

SHOPKEEPER: I've got mouse traps – they're just the thing,
                 A small bit of cheese and wind the spring.

DICK: It's poison I need, some rattle snake spit.
                 I can't catch an ant in a mouse trap, you twit.
                 I'll have half a pint of your deadliest brew
                 And while you're at it I'll have some cider, too.
                 Three flagons, some bread and some cheese
                 And, if it's no trouble, some chutney please.

SHOPKEEPER: Camel's green mucous and badger's bad breath,
                 One whiff of this means instant death.
                 Mind how you use it, it's powerful stuff,
                 Half a teaspoon's more than enough.

DICK: I'll take the bottleful, you can't be too sure,
                 Rodents these days are very mature.
                 That's the lot, there's no more to arrange,
                 Thanks very much – keep the change.

NARRATOR: Harry and Tom schemed all this time,
                 They thought they'd planned the perfect crime.
                 Foul and loathsome was their plot
                 And not a detail was forgot,
                 Two to one he'd be outnumbered.
                 With that cruel thought they gently slumbered,
                 As Dick returned to the oak by the wall.
                 His conscience disturbed him hardly at all,
                 With thoughts in his head of claiming the gold
                 Of poisoning his brothers and leaving them cold.
                 How innocent he looked that day,
                 Off for a picnic in the hay!
                 How healthy he seemed and how demure

But his mind was rotten as a sewer.
Just as he reached the other two
He knew what he'd forgot to do.
The poison he still had to share
And not wake up the sleeping pair.
(TOM and HARRY stir, but do not wake, as DICK pours poison into their cider jars)
He placed the drink beside each friend,
One sip of which would cause their end.
(DICK wakes them up)

DICK: A right pair of watchmen, you two make;
You can't even stay awake.
Here you are – there's cheese and bread,
Plenty of cider – a right royal spread.

TOM: Don't blame us, we were only snoozing.
What were you up to eh? I bet he was boozing.
TOM gives DICK a playful push – it develops into horseplay and then for real. DICK is murdered and TOM and HARRY are poisoned as they drink their wine.
The death scene is enacted in mime, possibly in silhouette behind a shadow-graph screen, possibly to a simple musical accompaniment of drum beat or tambourine)

NARRATOR: And so it happened, as had been planned,
That avarice destroyed the Avenging Band.
Little was said, save with Tom's dying breath

TOM: The old lady was right, we've all found Death.
(The three corpses turn to the audience, wearing "skull" masks. Old lady appears)

NARRATOR: Take heed you gamblers who lust after gold,
And you who insult ladies both young and old,
You drunkards and wasters, I cannot pretend
That it's likely you'll come to a pleasurable end.

The Merchant's Tale

NARRATOR:
In Lombardy, there's a place called Pavia.
Where once lived a knight of good behaviour,
Exceedingly rich, a bachelor bold,
Well on in age, seventy years old.
No wife in which his seed to sow,
And yet he was quite hetero.
On the shelf he was, high and dry,
His name was January – I don't know why.
One day he had a change of heart,
And summoned his friend, these words to impart.

JANUARY:
Dear Justinus, before it's too late,
I've decided I'm going to take me a mate.
I need a young wife to prove I'm a man,
I'm going to need all the help that I can.
And therefore, my friend, don't alter my course,
But give me assistance, my wishes endorse.

JUSTINUS:
I've known you well these many years

And though, not wishing to create fears,
I feel it my duty, as a friend,
To warn you of a possible end
To what you have proposed;
Not that I think the matter's closed.

JANUARY:
Come on Justinus, don't waffle about,
I don't see the problem, there's no cause for doubt.
What's left of my ardour, I don't want to waste it,
The pleasure of wedlock; I'm determined to taste it.
A strapping young wench, no more than twenty,
Someone like me who needs it plenty.
I want some fun and I want an heir,
I'm getting desperate for my share.

JUSTINUS:
A step like this needs rumination,
Meditation, consideration, reconsideration.

JANUARY:
Come to the point and say what you think
Before my vitals wither and shrink.

JUSTINUS:
In short, this advice I will impart –

Find out just if she's frigid – or a tart.
If she's a drunkard, or always in debt,
A gossip, maybe; but never forget
Married men do what they're told,
Bachelors are never made cuckold.
Nevertheless, if your mind is firm,
The wedding arrangements I will confirm.
Here's an instrument to improve your view,
There's the market place – it's up to you.
(JUSTINUS gives JANUARY a telescope. JANUARY scans audience. Ad lib remarks)

NARRATOR: Soon this January spied a maiden,
With shiny black curls her head was laden.
She'd a pert little nose and lovely big eyes,
And her other parts were of adequate size.
He considered her closely, the "That's" and the "This'es".
It was her he wanted for his missus.
(JUSTINUS prepares MAY for wedding ceremony)
The girl had barely a chance to speak,
The Wedding took place within the week.
Her name was May, her dowry small
But January wasn't bothered at all.
He signed to her his gold and land,
Overjoyed to have won her hand.
(Their hands are joined in marriage)
Guests from North, South, West and East
Joined the couple at the wedding feast.
Music played the whole night long,
Dancing, feasting, drink and song.
January gazed upon his bride
Anxious to be in bed by her side.
His heart beat fast his limbs were aching
For the love they'd soon be making.
She looked so frail, so chaste and demure,
Could she, he wondered, his ardours endure?
The night seemed long, it was nearly day,
He wished his guests would go away.
For them this was a night of fun;
For all, that is, excepting one.
His servant, Damian, faithful and true,
Never smiled the whole night through.
We'll talk of him later. Suffice to say
He was head over heels in love with May.
The guests, at last, to the door were led

And bride and bridegroom retired to bed.
(MAY gets into bed)
Before he climbed between the sheets,
He prepared himself for the treat of treats.
With perfumed stimulants his feet he dowsed,
Just to make sure she'd be aroused.
Tablets he swallowed and a bottle of tonic,
Guaranteed to make his parts bionic.
(MAY waits in bed, as JANUARY does physical exercises, runs round and over the bed etc. He jumps into bed)

JANUARY: O May, my sweet, my darling thing
            O what pleasure this night will bring.
            O what joy and what elation
            We'll have some fun and stimulation.
            (He kisses her and jumps out of bed. Tickles her feet. Stands on his head etc. or other eccentric business)

MAY: January, dear, all this to-ing and fro-ing
            Doesn't in the least bit get me going.

JANUARY: You're young, my dear, I know what I'm doing,
            You mustn't hurry when you're wooing.

MAY: I'm all for that, I'm in my prime,
            But how much longer? It's breakfast-time.

JANUARY: O goody, goody, breakfast in bed.
            One of the joys of being wed.
            (He opens packet of sandwiches)
            (Sings) "O what fun I've had in bed
            With the maid that I have wed.
            She's my Blossom and my May.
            She is mine all night and day."
            (JANUARY yawns, and falls fast asleep. MAY looks at him and does the same)

NARRATOR: And so we leave the newly wedded,
            Fast asleep and safely bedded;
            To observe poor Damian's pallid hue,
            Alas, his heart is broke in two.
            For four long day's he's kept his bed,
            While Eros fires at heart and head.
            There's only one thing on his mind –
            To lie with May, their limbs entwined.

He writes a couplet, then a stanza;
And puts it to music, like Mario Lanza.

DAMIAN: "May, you shine just like the moon,
That is why I've wrote this tune.
My heart it aches, I'm feeling blue,
All that matters is just us two.
I cannot help the way I feel,
At your feet I wish to kneel.
I want to kiss and hold you tight,
Please think of me in bed tonight.
With love for you I'm badly hit.
Don't tell anyone what I've writ."
(DAMIAN groans as JANUARY and others try to cheer him up)

NARRATOR: No one could his anguish ease,
They thought he had a strange disease.
They did their best, his heart beat faster.
They gave him tablets and a sticking plaster.

JANUARY: Damian, dear lad, where's the pain?
Down there? I see. Perhaps it's a sprain.
It's not mentioned in the medical book,
I'll ask my bride to have a look.
(JANUARY calls MAY. She enters in her night dress. DAMIAN
groans even more)

JANUARY: May, my dear, come here awhile,
Look at Damian; give him a smile.
Perhaps to see your face so pure
Will prove to be the only cure.
(MAY looks at DAMIAN, then peers under the bed clothes)

MAY: What's wrong with him I'm shy of telling,
He has a most unnatural swelling.
The only hope is careful feeding,
Ice-cold baths and bible-reading.

NARRATOR: Without a single person knowing,
Damian deftly passed his poem.
In May the young lad placed his trust,
As she popped it down her bust.
(MAY and JANUARY leave DAMIAN)
The couple then to bed retired
As he his passions stoked and fired.

(Same business as before. JANUARY swallowing pills, jumping over bed etc. He goes to sleep)
At last, sweet May could find the time
To read poor Damian's amorous rhyme.
When she read of the love-sick poet,
She was filled with pity, but couldn't show it.
For January was soon awake,
And a hasty action she had to take.

JANUARY: Goody, goody, goody, breakfast in bed
One of the joys of being wed.
(MAY hides the note in a sandwich and gives it to JANUARY. He eats it and goes back to sleep. MAY creeps out of bed and whispers to DAMIAN through the wall)

MAY: Damian, dear, can you hear my voice?
(He gets out of bed and taps on the wall in acknowledgement)
I'd like to help but we've got no choice.
I give you my word, when the time is right,
That in my arms I'll hold you tight.
I beg you, please, upon my knee
Please cheer up and trust in me.

NARRATOR: Damian's recovery was now complete,
He was back to work and on his feet.
O, happy for this writer of verse!
While January took a turn for the worse.
A few weeks later, O dreadful plight!
His eyes went dim; he lost his sight.
No longer could he see his bride,
And so he kept her to his side.
With jealousy his heart did burn
Lest from himself her eyes might turn.
He held her hand both night and day
And Damian couldn't get near to May.
(MAY leads JANUARY by the hand, as DAMIAN watches)
Now, in a part of his estate
Was a high walled garden with a gate.
Concealed it was from human view
Where they would sport the whole night through.
What games they'd play these newly-weds,
Romping in the flower-beds.
The gate was locked with a single key
And that was kept by January.
But May had had a subtle plan

To make a cuckold of her old man.
With a piece of soft wax very delicately
She'd taken a cast for a duplicate key.
This she tossed to her young admirer
With a promise that he would soon acquire her,
If in the bushes he would hide
And wait till she was by his side.
(*DAMIAN blows kiss. Exits*)

MAY: It's stuffy inside on this hot summer's day,
       I wish I could cool myself some way.

JANUARY: I've got an idea that cannot wait,
       I'll open up the garden gate.
       We'll have some fun with the flowers and fruits.
       And run about in our birthday suits.
       O goody, goody, good.
       (*MAY and JANUARY exit*)

NARRATOR: This garden gave complete seclusion,
       Compete that is, with one exclusion.
       For some there are, as free as air is,
       Ah yes, you've guessed, our friends, the fairies.
       (*Enter PLUTO and PROSERPINE, King and Queen of the Fairies. They have wings strapped to their backs, and wear tights and tutus. They each carry a wand containing star-dust*)
       Here they are, the King and Queen,
       More enchanting, you've never seen.
       When either sun or moon did shine
       Came Pluto and his Proserpine.
       Invisible to human eye,
       They could run, dance and even fly.
       (*As PROSERPINE and PLUTO dance and flap their wings – they notice DAMIAN enter and hide behind a bush*)

PROSERPINE: Pluto, dear, did you see that?
       He's up to something, I smell a rat.
       That was Damian, I know his face,
       He shouldn't be here in this private place.

PLUTO: Suspicious thoughts can be misleading.
       Perhaps it's the gardener doing the weeding.
       (*JANUARY and MAY enter*)

JANUARY: If my presence seems over-zealous,

It's because my blindness makes me jealous.
And, therefore, do not grieve, my wife,
If I ask you to be true for life,
And faithful, as all wives should.
I promise it's for your own sweet good.
In the eyes of God you will be pure,
And your own honour will be secure.
And thirdly, if you pledge yourself,
You'll have my land and all my wealth.

MAY:
I never thought you'd ever doubt me
Or think suspiciously about me.
When I married you, I bade my troth
And I'm not one to break my oath.
It's women always get the blame
The men are innocent – always the same.
(She weeps and signals to DAMIAN, indicating that he climb up into a tree)

NARRATOR:
To hear his wife sound so offended
Was not what January had intended.
And so he consoled her tenderly
While Damian got ready in the tree.
(JANUARY consoles MAY, as Damian's clothes fall from the tree)

PLUTO:
Did you hear that hussy? I've had enough,
I'm not going to watch this filthy stuff.
The man's been wronged but he can't see
Something's up in that there tree.
It's just like women to tell those lies,
It's most offensive to fairies' eyes.
I've got a plan to put things right,
I'm going to give him back his sight!

PROSERPINE:
Don't blame the girl, and don't dare scold,
He thinks he's bought her with his gold.
Creepy old man with withered-up skin,
Why should she be in love with him?
Her feelings have been tied and trussed
To satisfy an old man's lust.
She's a woman, dear, in her own right,
And I promise, if you give him his sight,
Your magic will be of little use
Because I'll give her a good excuse.

59

MAY: January, dear, come here awhile
                All is forgiven, please give me a smile.
                It's pleasant in the summer breeze
                Standing underneath these trees.
                Would you like some fruit? There's some up there,
                I can see an enormous juicy pear.

JANUARY: I'd pick it myself for you, dear
                Or ask Damian to, if he were here.
                You'll have to climb upon my back.
                That's it. It's easy once you get the knack.

NARRATOR: She got the knack and plenty more,
                As Damian thrust like a rampant boar.
                In all the orchards lush and green,
                Never has fruit like this been seen.
                Just as they reached the height of joy
                Pluto waved his magic toy.
                (PLUTO sprinkles star-dust on JANUARY)

JANUARY: Have you got it dear? Are you alright?
                That's funny, everything's turning bright.
                (He looks up into the tree)
                Good God!
                So this is how my wife deceives!
                Jumping with Damian among the leaves.
                Stop that at once, you filthy flirts!
                Or else I'll hit you where it hurts.
                For this disgusting recreation
                I think you owe an explanation.

NARRATOR: That's surprised these two love-birds,
                See how May is lost for words.
                But not for long is she left to stutter
                As Proserpine gives her words to utter.

MAY: I don't think I like your attitude,
                That's a fine way to show your gratitude!
                It's due to a dream I had last night,
                That I have just restored your sight.
                You've got your sight back, thanks to me.
                I was told to fight Damian in a tree.

JANUARY: Don't give me that fiddle-faddle,
                I saw him riding, in the saddle.

What a ridiculous anecdote!
I haven't come off a banana-boat.

MAY: You've got your sight back – that is true,
The rest you've imagined – it isn't new.
Always when men recover their sight
They don't at first quite see aright.
Forget whatever you thought you saw,
It's your imagination – nothing more.
Be thankful you've been blessed in life
With a faithful, true, devoted wife.
To say those things is very hateful.
You really seem to be ungrateful.
(She weeps)

JANUARY: I'm sorry dear for what I thought,
The sudden brightness made me fraught.
I see now what you said is true;
To you and Damian, my thanks are due.

NARRATOR: And so ends the tale of a man and his bride.
Some will take hers, and others, his side.
I'll take the simplest way there is,
And leave it to those scheming fairies.

PLUTO: Listen, you men, whatever you do,
Never trust women to be faithful to you.
They'll lie and deceive you with dirty tricks,
Just so as they can get their kicks.

PROSERPINE: Well, that's a charming thing to tell,
And quite untrue, as you know well.
If men want our body without our mind,
They'll be paid back in their own kind.

NARRATOR: A word of advice, begging your pardon.
Beware of fairies in your garden.

M.C: Thank you, ladies and gentlemen, that concludes this evening's entertainment. Without further ado, the finalists will line up and we'll get on with the judging.

MILLER: I haven't told my Medieval Top Ten number one.

M.C: So what?

MILLER: You said I could tell all ten. I've only told nine.

M.C: I never said anything of the sort.

MILLER: You did. You said I could tell my Medieval top ten.

M.C: While the others were preparing to tell their tales.
(General argument. M.C. calms everyone down)
Never let it be said that I am not a man of my word. *(To audience)* I do apologise. Well, go on, your number one.

MILLER: Right. Top of the Medieval hit parade for the last 600 years, "The Miller'sTale" by Geoffrey Chaucer.

M.C: I've told you a thousand times, that tale has been disqualified.

MILLER: It's my number one, and you just said I could tell my number one.
(Another general argument)

M.C: Wait a minute, wait a minute! *(silence)* There is only one thing to do in these circumstances, and that is to ask them. *(To audience)* Now, ladies and gentlemen, surely you don't wish to witness the Miller's Tale?

AUDIENCE: Yes!!

M.C: You do? Very well, on your own heads be it. The Miller's Tale. But don't say I didn't warn you.

The Miller's Tale

M.C.:   He told his tale in his own vulgar way,
I apologise for repeating it here today.
So to those with delicate taste, I pray
For the love of God, don't think that what I say
Is of evil intent, for I must rehearse
Every single tale, for better or worse,
Exactly as told, or else tell lies.
Those who might take offence would be wise
To turn the page and choose another sort
They're all here, clean or dirty, long or short

Oh, wait a minute. There's something written at the bottom of the page. It's in Old English. I think it's Geoffrey Chaucer's handwriting.

If the filth of the Miller
Ye find far too candid
Please writte ye not
To the Evening Standard.
(*N.B. The above to be adapted to accommodate the name of a local paper*)

MILLER: There was this rich geezer called John,
Quite old, well, he was getting on.
By trade he was a Carpenter;
He took a young wench and he married her.
You'd think at his age he'd had enough,
Because this Alison was a tasty bit of stuff.
He bought lots of clothes to impress her,
Because Al was a real natty dresser.
Shapely too, with a lecherous eye
Which she used to wink at passers-by.
Now they let out a room to a youth,
A lad named Nicholas, very couth.
He knew a lot about the stars;
Predictions, the weather and isobars.
He could forecast rain, he could forecast snow,
He was meteorologically in the know.
There was one thing on the mind of this weather guesser.
Young Alison had given him a ridge of high pressure.
And to tell the truth
He was a sly and randy youth.

NICHOLAS: By all the sun and moon and stars,
              Look at Alison's shapely hips.
              I'd like to touch her back and front,
              I wouldn't half like to kiss her lips.

ALISON: I'm so fed up it's disconcerting,
              To think that I could be out flirting.
              I don't enjoy these household chores,
              Washing stairs and scrubbing floors.
              My John's too old to be my lover,
              All I am's his full time scrubber.

NICHOLAS: (Creeps up behind her) Oh what a face! what a figure!
              Part of me is getting bigger.
              I'll creep up on her from behind,
              I bet she likes the other kind.

ALISON: How dare you grope, you naughty knave!
              I really think you should behave.
              You know my husband's out at work,
              If he finds out he'll go berserk.

NICHOLAS: Don't tell him Alison, my pet,
              You're the hottest thing I've ever met.
              I tell the truth it's not a lie,
              I must have you or I'll die.

ALISON: Oh, Nicholas you poor dear thing!
              Not now, I heard the doorbell ring.
              I promise you I'll make a date,
              Some other time, we'll have to wait.
              (She answers the door)

ABSALOM: Good afternoon, my precious pet,
              Oh my dear young lady, I'm glad we've met.
              I've watched you in church at evensong;
              I swing the incense, the name's Absalom.
              I have an ecclesiastical obsession,
              Can I hear your latest confession?

ALISON: Not today, thank you. Can you come back when my
              husband's in?

ABSALOM: Can I come when her husband's in?
              I'll have a go, though it is a sin.

With her I really could go far,
I'll just nip back for my guitar.
(Exit)

NICHOLAS: Dear Alison, I have a plan
To outwit the likes of your old man.
I'll pretend to be ill for a day or two,
So bring up some booze and plenty of stew.
(Exit to bedroom)

JOHN: *(Entering)* Alison! Alison!! Yoo hoo. Alison!
I'm home, my love, my dear, my sweet!
I'm starving, what've you got to eat?
Is there some bread or cheese or pickles?
By the way, have you seen young Nickles?

ALISON: Funny you should say that, my dear John,
I don't quite know what's going on.
His bedroom door's not made a squeak,
Why not slip up and take a peek?
(JOHN creeps up to Nicholas' room – hammers on the door)

JOHN: Hullo, Nicholas, are you alright?
The door seems to be shut tight

ALISON: Look through the keyhole, husband dear,
Something's up, that seems quite clear.
(JOHN looks through keyhole)

JOHN: He's lying stretched out on the floor!
Come girl, help break down the door.
(They burst into room)
Nicholas, are you alright?
By heck, he's looking white.
What on earth can have occurred?
Say something, lad, just one word.

NICHOLAS: Pollux!

JOHN: What's that, son, are you in pain?
I didn't quite hear, say it again.

NICHOLAS: Pollux.

JOHN: I thought that's what you said.

Do you feel alright in the head?

NICHOLAS: Castor and Pollux, the heavenly pair,
Messages of doom in the ethereal air.

JOHN: I see, you've been over-working, perhaps.
Take it easy, it must be a relapse.

NICHOLAS: I was holding my astrolabe in my hands
When suddenly it struck me in the glands.
All is clear, only I can see,
Inter-globular cosmography.
What I know and what I've felt,
To me the cards of wisdom have been dealt.
Photospheres and astromography,
The crab's in Venus. O Catastrophe!

JOHN: What's that? What's happened?

NICHOLAS: I cannot say, my lips are sealed,
Only to me is the truth revealed.
O, Calamity!

JOHN: Tell you what, I'll forget last week's rent.
Now what's new in the firmament?
Something's happening isn't it, lad?
I hope it isn't anything bad.

NICHOLAS: O catastrophe!

JOHN: Come on Nicholas, I won't tell.

NICHOLAS: O yes you will.

JOHN: O no I won't.

NICHOLAS: O yes you will.

JOHN: O no I won't.

NICHOLAS: *(And audience)* O, yes you will!

JOHN: O, give us a break.
I promise on the word of God,
Now, come on Nicholas, you rotten sod.

NICHOLAS: Very well, but God will strike you dead,
If you repeat one word of what I've said.

JOHN: Cross my heart and hope to die,
Your secret's safe, I tell no lie.

NICHOLAS: This is the truth that I have found,
There'll be a flood, we'll all be drowned.
It is the will of God on High
To pour down water from the sky.
O Calamity!

JOHN: When is this flood? When is it due?
It's come as a shock; I'm telling you.

NICHOLAS: Tonight's the night the flood will rise,
We'll all be in it, up to our eyes.

JOHN: What can we do to stop from drowning?
I'm overwrought, it's quite astounding.

NICHOLAS: There is a way to save us three;
Follow the instructions carefully.
Fetch three baskets or wooden boxes;
We must be cunning though, like foxes.
No one must know what you're after,
And when you've got them, hang them from the rafter.

JOHN: Hang them up in the ceiling? Why?
NICHOLAS: To question the heavens would be profaneness,
These messages come direct from Uranus.
So hurry up. There's no time to lose,
And you'd better bring some food and lots of booze.

JOHN: O, I see. I'll just pop out, secretly.
No one will know, just us three
(He exits and bumps into ABSALOM)

ABSALOM: Hullo, John, What's going on?

What're you popping out secretly for?

JOHN: Tonight's the night I'll say no more. *(Exit)*

ABSALOM: "Tonight's the night", I heard him say!

When she hears my song, I'll be well away.
I'll have a little practice here and now,
(*Italian serenade as baskets, boxes or whatever are prepared*)

JOHN: I've fetched three baskets deep and wide
            And packed some food supplies inside.
            But are you sure it'll rain tonight?
            There hasn't been a cloud in sight.

NICHOLAS: Of course I'm sure, now just keep calm.
            In these boats we're safe from harm.
            Come on, John, no hesitation,
            Get in and pray for our salvation.
            (*They get in baskets. JOHN prays quietly to himself.*)

JOHN: To me this all seems a bit funny,
            The weather forecast's dry and sunny.

NICHOLAS: That's why no one else is ready.
            Now go to sleep and take it steady.
            Goodnight John, Goodnight Nicholas etc. etc. (*all saying
            'Goodnight' to each other*)
            (*ABSALOM enters, playing loud music*)

JOHN: Who is making all that noise?
            It must be one of those delinquent boys
            (*Shouts*) Go away you noisy youth
            I want some sleep and that's the truth.
            (*Throws wellie at him*)

ABSALOM: (*Smells wellie*)
            That must be Alison's husband John.
            I think I'll come back later on,
            When he's asleep, and all is still,
            I'll creep up to her windowsill. (*Exits*)
            (*JOHN nods off to sleep – snoring loudly. NICHOLAS and
            ALISON climb out, stealthily, and get into bed. ABSALOM re-
            enters.*)
            Alison my dove, it's me!
            Return my love, I'm on my knee.

ALISON: Absalom, please go away!
            It's with another I wish to lay.
            You'll wake my husband from his slumber,
            Then we all will be in lumber.

ABSALOM: Please give me one small kiss,
Then I'll be off, I truly promise.

ALISON: O, alright.
(*Long silence, then giggles as she whispers a plan in NICHOLAS' ear*)

ABSALOM: Alison, me knee's hurting.

ALISON: On condition that you go,
I'll put my face out of the window.

ABSALOM: O, she's going to put her face out of the window!
I can't wait.
(*ABSALOM demonstrates what he will do in kissing her face. She sticks her bum out of the window. Or failing that, a pair of balloons inside flesh-coloured tights*)
That's her face in the gloom!
In this light it looks just like the moon.
(*Kissing business*)
I feel your cheeks though I cannot see,
Your sweet breath is life perfume to me.
My tongue it tingles, you taste so lovely.
Funny though, your chin feels stubbly.
I've kissed her bum, the dirty cow!
I'll get my own back. I know how.
(*Exit*) (*ALISON back to bed*)

NICHOLAS: Before we have another go
I'll just point percy at the po.
(*NICHOLAS relieves himself in chamber pot. ABSALOM re-enters with red-hot poker*)

ABSALOM: She thinks she's a joker.
Just wait till she feels my red hot poker.
Alison! I've got a gift for you!
Please kiss once again, oh do.

NICHOLAS: (*Female voice*) I'm coming!

ABSALOM: O, she's coming. She's coming.
(*NICHOLAS sticks his bum out of the window*)

ABSALOM: Speak pretty girl and say where thou art. (*A loud fart*)
She's let out a dirty great fart. Take that!

(*ABSALOM strikes NICHOLAS on the bum with poker*)

NICHOLAS: Water! Water!
(*JOHN wakes up*)

JOHN: Water, water, did he say?
The flood has come – we must away!
(*He cuts line holding his basket and crashes down*)

ABSALOM: A flood, you fool? You've gone insane.
It's three months since we had rain.

JOHN: He told me it was in the stars,
By Uranus out of Mars.

NICHOLAS: You keep my anus out of this (*Sits on pot*)
O, Thank the Lord I had a piss.

ABSALOM: So at last it's come to pass,
You've been branded on the arse.

NICHOLAS: Well, you're a right one, Holy Clerk,
Kissing hairy bums in the dark!

ALISON: Poor dear Nicholas, he caught you bending.
He's given you an unhappy ending.

M.C: Thus swyved was this carpenter's wife
For all his keeping and his jealousy.
And Absalom has kissed her nether-eye
And Nicholas is scalded in the toute.
The tale is done, and God save all the rowte!
(*After the Miller's Tale the M.C. calls the company together for the judging, presenting them in turn to the audience. Maybe there's a rudimentary 'clapometer' to record the applause. The Miller is not included, his tale not being part of the official competition. Naturally he complains. The M.C. eventually concedes (e.g. "If you can face the embarrassment, let's see what the audience think of you") The Miller claims the cup, to the annoyance of the other competitors.*)